HOSPITAL FARM

Silly Goose Chase

This book belongs to...

....

Silly Goose Chase

Written by Jackie Andrews
Illustrated by Jacqueline East

Bright ☆ Sparks

This is Haven Farm Animal Hospital.

It's a special place for animals in need of care.

Joe and Sally live here, with Mum, Dad,
Patch the dog and Tabby the cat.

Dad is a vet. He helps the sick animals to get better.

Mum runs the farm.

Joe and Sally help with the farm and care for the animals.

One morning, Dad came out of his surgery with something large, white and noisy in his arms.

"Oh, wow! Is that a goose?" asked Joe.

"Yes, Joe," said Dad, trying not to get a mouthful of feathers! "Her wing is damaged, but I think she'll be fine, with a little rest."

"Where will she live?" asked Sally.

"Well, I'll put her with the ducks for now," said Dad,
"but I expect she'll soon decide where *she* wants to go."

The young goose swam in the duck pond, honking *very* loudly.

"Do you think she'll keep that noise up forever?" asked Sally, covering her ears with her hands.

"At least we know what to call her," said Joe. "Noisy!" Sally laughed and Noisy the goose honked even louder.

Next, Noisy decided to explore the duck house. One or two ducks flew out in a hurry. Then, she tried to squeeze out again – she hadn't found anything to interest her!

"Oh, no! Look, Joe!" cried Sally.

Noisy couldn't get out of the duck house! And it didn't matter how much she honked, she was stuck tight!

The children managed to free Noisy and carefully gave her a clean. It took them ages and, as soon as they had finished, the goose waddled away from the pond to explore some of the farm buildings.

"Come on, Sally," said Joe. "We'd better catch her, before she gets into any *more* trouble!"

Sure enough, Noisy pushed open the door to the dairy and went inside.

By the time Joe and Sally got there, she had already gobbled up some butter and cheese and knocked over a pail of milk!

"Oh, no!" cried Joe and Sally, as they saw all the mess Noisy had made.

This time, it took them even longer to clean the naughty goose and the dairy. Mum wasn't happy with Noisy at all!

"That naughty goose will have to go back to the duck pond," she told Joe and Sally, as they cleaned up the mess.

Soon, the dairy was clean once again.

"Where is Noisy now?" asked Mum.

Joe and Sally looked at each other.
Then, they looked around the dairy.

Suddenly, they all heard a faint honking noise.

"That sounds like she's found the stables,"
said Sally. "Come on, Joe!"

Joe and Sally ran as fast as they could to the stables.
Hearing the noise, Old Major looked over his stall.
This silly goose chase looked like great fun!

"Honk! Honk!" went the
naughty goose.

"She's in the tack room!" cried Joe. This was where
they kept the saddles and bridles for the horses
and all the cleaning equipment.

They found Noisy tangled up in tack, leather polish and dusters, trying to eat one of the grooming brushes!

"Oh, no!" said Sally. "She's knocked everything down from the shelves. It's going to take ages to put everything away again."

Joe and Sally rescued Noisy from the tangle. They took away the grooming brush and put her into an empty horse box, while they tidied the tack room.

However, Noisy didn't want to be shut away. There were lots more places she wanted to explore!

"Phew! I don't know about you, Joe," said Sally, "but I'm getting really tired!"

"Well, she's safe in the box now," said Joe. "Besides, there aren't any other places she can go, are there?"

Then, they both had the same idea – the store room!

Too late! Noisy had already escaped!

The store room at Haven Farm was where they did the washing, kept the coal and firewood, stored bags of dried food for Patch and Tabby and lots of other things.

Noisy found it *so* exciting. There were lots of interesting smells and she couldn't resist trying a little bit of this and a little bit of that!

When Joe and Sally arrived, Noisy the goose was covered in coal dust, washing powder and dried food!

"Noisy!" groaned the children.

"Miaow!" went Tabby the cat.

"Honk! Honk!" called Noisy, cheerfully.

This time, Mum helped Joe and Sally to clear up.

"We'll just have to make sure all the doors are fastened," said Mum. "She'll get tired of exploring, eventually. It must all be very new for her."

"You'd think she'd be tired now," said Sally. "I am!"

They all laughed. Suddenly, Joe stopped smiling.

"Where is she?" he asked, horrified.

Noisy had waddled round the side of the house and discovered a new place, full of interesting things.

Dad had just parked his tractor and left the barn doors open. Noisy slipped inside, honking curiously – where should she start?

She poked her head between the tins on the shelf. Then, she hopped onto the bench and pecked at some tools, an oily cloth and a big sponge in a yellow bucket.

Then, a box of shiny nuts and bolts caught her eye...

"Noisy! Here, goosey, goosey!" called Joe and Sally. They looked everywhere, but couldn't find the silly goose.

Patch the dog came along to help, trotting round the farm, his nose to the ground.

"It's funny we can't hear her any more," said
Sally. "Do you think something's happened?"

Suddenly, Patch picked up the goose's scent
and ran ahead, barking.

"Look!" said Joe. "Patch is heading for the barn."

And inside the barn, they found Noisy looking really sorry for herself. Beside her was a nearly empty nuts and bolts tin!

With a bit of a struggle, Joe and Sally grabbed Noisy and quickly took her to the surgery.

Once there, they told Dad all about the silly goose chase.

'I can give her some medicine, which will help get rid of all those nuts and bolts," said Mr Haven.

"With any luck, we won't need to operate on her. But I'll keep her safe, here in the hospital, until tomorrow!"

Luckily for Noisy, Dad's medicine worked and Noisy was soon feeling *much* better.

"Do you think she's learnt her lesson?" asked Sally, when they were all having breakfast one morning.

"Oh, yes," said Mum, smiling. "She knows just where to go for the right kind of food now!"

"Honk! Honk!"

Joe and Sally looked round. There, at the door, was Noisy – waiting for Mum to give her a bowl of grain and some vegetables.

"She's not such a silly goose after all!" laughed Joe.

Bright ★ Sparks

Thank you for buying this Bright Sparks book.

We donate one book to less fortunate children for every two sold.
We have already donated over 150,000 books.

We want to help the world to read.

This is a Bright Sparks book
First published in 2002
Bright Sparks, Queen Street House,
4 Queen Street, BATH BA1 1HE, UK
Copyright © Parragon 2002

Created and produced by
The Complete Works
St Mary's Road,
Royal Leamington Spa,
Warwickshire CV31 1JP, UK

Printed in China
ISBN 1-84250-408-8